New York is a mysterious city, and that's just above ground. Things are even stranger in the tangle of sewers under the streets. If you dare to know more, read on . . .

Copyright © 2007 by NordSüd Verlag AG, Zürich, Switzerland
First published in Switzerland under the title *Mike O'Hara und die Alligatoren von New York*
English translation copyright © 2007 by North-South Books Inc., New York

First published in the United States, Great Britain, Canada, Australia, and New Zealand in 2007 by North-South Books Inc., an imprint of NordSüd Verlag AG, Zürich, Switzerland. Distributed in the United States by North-South Books Inc., New York.

Library of Congress Cataloging-in-Publication Data is available.
A CIP catalogue record for this book is available from The British Library.

ISBN-13: 978-0-7358-2124-8 / ISBN-10: 0-7358-2124-0 (trade edition)
10 9 8 7 6 5 4 3 2 1

Printed in Belgium

Alligator Mike

By Jürg Federspiel
Illustrated by Petra Rappo

NORTHSOUTH
BOOKS
New York / London

One day, Mike was chasing
his ball when it bounced into
a garbage can. Not thinking,
Mike dove in after it, headfirst.

Oddly, the garbage can didn't have a bottom. Mike plummeted straight down a tunnel, deep into the underground world beneath the city.

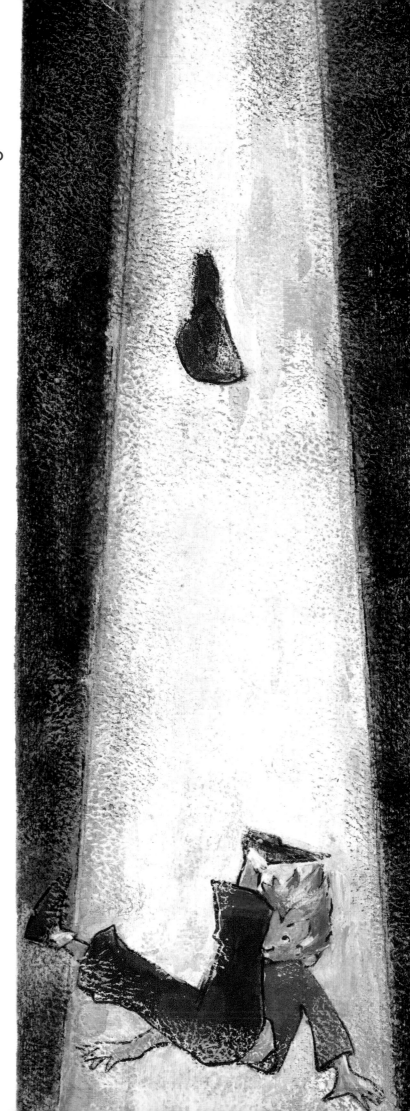

Luckily, he landed on a pile of old mattresses so he didn't get hurt. Still, he was a little nervous when he heard a squeaky voice ask: "Who are you?"

"Uh . . . my name's Mike," he said.

A head slowly bounced into view, followed by a body.

"Hello, Mike. My name is Balloonhead. Everyone calls me Balbo for short."

"Do you live here?" asked Mike

"Yup, yup," said Balbo. "These tunnels are my home!"

"Are you all alone down here?" said Mike.

"No, no!" Balbo bounced to the edge of the light and called, "Come out, you guys. It's okay. It's just a boy named Mike."

Four more odd characters came out of the darkness and smiled at Mike. They looked like they were made of random leftover things. One looked a little like a dog. Suddenly, they all started talking at once.

"A boy!"

"Are you a real boy?"

"Named Mike?"

"You live aboveground?"

Mike nodded. "Why?" he asked.

"We need your help!"

"Come!"

"Follow us!"

"Let's go," said Balbo, and Mike followed them, feeling a bit like he was in a crazy parade.

They led him down dark tunnels that were full of pipes and water mains. Way overhead Mike could hear the screech and rumble of subway cars taking normal people normal places.

Up ahead, he saw a sewer pipe with platforms on each side.
As he came closer, he was shocked to see that on the platforms
were . . .

. . . hundreds of alligators! On one side of the canal, the alligators were green. On the other, they were a ghostly white.

All of them were dressed up elegantly, with jewelry and hats and pocketbooks and parasols. Everything they wore looked a little battered, as if it had been found in the sewers.

And all of them were angry. They shouted insults across the water and threw rubbish at each other.

"Intruders!" shouted the white alligators.

"Lazy loafers! Stingy!"
screamed the green alligators.
They lashed their tails on
the platforms so that it
sounded like a battle.

"What's the problem?" asked Mike, who could barely hear above the noise.

"They are fighting over who gets to eat the stale bagels and muffins and who gets to sleep near the water," answered Balbo. "The white ones have been here in the dark so long that they have lost their green color. The green ones are newer arrivals."

"But where do they come from?"

"Their home is in the swamps of Florida, but tourists brought them back as babies. They found their way into the drains and ended up here. None of them are happy, and they fight all the time."

"Why don't they go back to Florida?" Mike asked.

"They would if they could, but they can't."

"Of course they can," Mike said. "My uncle runs a shipping company. He takes passengers up and down the coast all the time. All they have to do is pay for the passage." Mike stopped as he realized something. "Oh," he said, "they don't have any money."

"Money?" said Balbo. "That's all? That's not a problem!"

"What do you mean?" Mike asked. "They are alligators, living in sewers!"

Balbo bounced up toward the furious, snapping alligators. "Listen, all of you!" he cried. "Do you want to go back to Florida?"

All the alligators looked up in silence at Balbo.

"Listen to what this boy has to say."

Hundreds of glittering eyes turned to stare at Mike. Their jewelry and ragtag clothing did not quite conceal their wicked sharp teeth and claws.

"Ummm, I think I know how you can get back to Florida," Mike began nervously.

A rumble of approval rang through the long tunnel.

"You could go there on my uncle's ship. But," he hesitated, looking at all those teeth, "you'll need a lot of money."

A long pause followed. Then came a joyous riot. The alligators had not dreamed that they would ever get out of this sewer. The only thing between them and their beloved swamp was money. And that was something people lost down drainpipes on a daily basis! Coins, jewels, even gold watches.

An elegant female alligator ripped off her pearl necklace and threw it at Mike's feet.

"Hurrah!" shouted the others, and they all followed her example.

Jewels, gold coins, walking sticks, silk shawls, baby clothes, ties, shoes—everything they wore and everything they had hoarded away—all of it flew through the air and landed at Mike's feet. Soon the pile became a mountain.

"I'll leave the clothes," Mike said, surveying the lot. "But the money and pearls and diamonds are good." He took all the jewels and coins and put them into a suitcase.

The suitcase was heavy. That's when Mike remembered how he'd gotten there in the first place.
"How will I ever get above ground again?"

"Don't worry," Balbo said and winked at him. "There is a service entrance."

Mike climbed the ladder with the suitcase in one hand,
pushed up the manhole cover, and ended up back on the street.
The creature who looked a little like a dog accompanied him.

When he looked around,
he saw that he was already in
Uncle Ernie's neighborhood.

Uncle Ernie was surprised when he opened his door and saw Mike. Then he shook his head and said, "Please come in!"

Mike handed his uncle the suitcase.

"Holy mackerel," said his uncle. "What an incredible treasure. Where did you find it?"

Mike told his uncle all about the alligators in the sewers. "All they need is passage on a ship back to Florida," he finished. "Do you think this will be enough?"

Uncle Ernie scratched his chin and thought long and hard. Finally he asked, "How many alligators are there?"

"Three hundred and thirty," said Mike. "I counted."

When they traded in the treasure
for cash, it was more than enough
to pay for passage for all the
alligators and food for the trip
besides.

The following night, while everyone
else in the city was sleeping, Mike
went to get the alligators.

Three hundred and thirty silent alligators tiptoed through the streets to the pier where they boarded the ship.

Uncle Ernie gave the captain explicit instructions to let the alligators off in Florida on the edge of a large swamp.